This igloo book belongs to:

....

Published in 2019
by Igloo Books Ltd
Cottage Farm
Sywell
NN6 0BJ
www.igloobooks.com

GUA006 0119
6 8 10 9 7
ISBN 978-1-78670-142-8

Written by Sienna Williams
Illustrated by Steven Wood

Cover designed by Lee Italiano & Justine Ablett
Interiors designed by Justine Ablett
Edited by Stephanie Moss

Printed and manufactured in China

igloobooks

There was a rubber duck,
with a little orange beak.
"I wish that I could fly,"
he said sadly, with a squeak.

When he saw the real birds, he thought,
"That's the life for me."
He stared through the bathroom window
and dreamed of flying free.

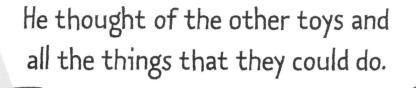

He thought of the other toys and
all the things that they could do.

Space Alien had a
cool ship that

F L A S H E D

purple and then blue!

Monkey had long arms for swinging.

Race Car whizzed and went

ZOOM!

All Rubber Duck could do was bob alone in the bathroom.

The other toys all smiled kindly and said,
**"But rubber ducks don't fly!
You're made for splashing at bath time,
but of course we'll help you try."**

"Have you tried flapping your wings?"
asked Monkey, with a cheeky smile.

He replied that his little wings
couldn't take him half a mile.

"Rubber Duck," said Race Car next, "climb up onto my back.
If I drive super-quick, maybe you'll fly off the track!"

So they whizzed round
and round, till Race Car
ran out of puff.
"Nice try," said Rubber Duck,
"but it wasn't fast enough!"

Last, it was Space Alien who was sure he was up to the task.
"Let's use my flying spaceship," he said.
"All you have to do is ask!"

He started pushing buttons.

BEEP,

RUMBLE, CLICK!

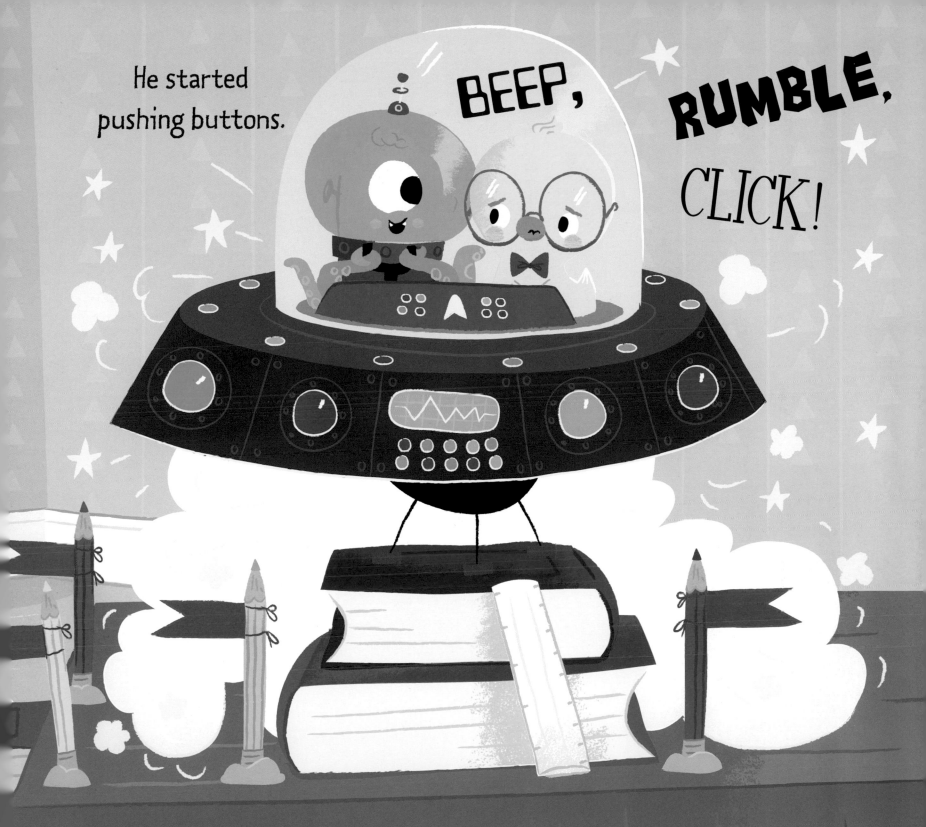

"Please stop!" said Rubber Duck. "I think I feel sick!"

Rubber Duck splashed in the bath, feeling sadder than ever.

So the toys all gathered round and put their heads together.

"We've got to find a way to help," said Teddy. "We can't quit now. Rubber Duck has to learn to fly and I think that I know how."

His friends all gathered supplies and then set to work straight away.

When Rubber Duck saw what they'd built, he didn't know what to say.

"Sit on this toy-block see-saw.
We'll jump on it from the bed."

"**Then you'll** WHOOSH **into the sky,**" all his clever toy friends said.

Rubber Duck settled in place and sat down with a **bump**.

Then the toys all counted down, "Ready? 1... 2... 3...

JUMP!"

Rubber Duck soared up and up, as his friends all clapped and cheered.

But being up so high was SCARIER than he'd ever feared!

Rubber Duck felt terrified.
He made a loud quacking sound.
He flew through the air.
Then he bumped back to the ground.

"Again?" asked the toys, as he
gave his rubber tail a shake.
How could he tell all his friends that
he'd made such a mistake?

"I don't think flying is for me," he said. "**Maybe I was wrong.**"
"**We know,**" they said, kindly.
"**You belonged in the bath all along.**"

Through a beak full of bubbles he thanked them
for everything they'd tried.
Before he knew it, the toys jumped in, too.
"Pool party!" they all cried.